Mercer Mayer's
Herbert the Timid Dragon

To Carolyn Skiles,
who is not so timid anymore

Mercer Mayer's
Herbert the Timid Dragon

A GOLDEN BOOK • NEW YORK

Western Publishing Company, Inc., Racine, Wisconsin 53404

Herbert the dragon lived in a snug cave at the edge of the wild forest. Every night at bedtime, Herbert read a story from his favorite book, *Knights in Armor*. He loved the exciting tales of brave knights and princesses in distress.

"I wish I were a brave knight in armor," thought Herbert.

But Herbert wasn't brave. As a matter of fact, Herbert was timid. You might even say he was afraid of his own shadow.

Even so, Herbert decided one day to leave home and seek adventure as a knight. He packed his bag and started out along the dusty road.

HERBERT

He hadn't gone far when he came
upon a broken-down carriage and a
princess in distress.

"Oh, boy!" thought Herbert. "This is
my first chance to act like a knight."

"May I help?" Herbert asked.

The men fixing the carriage didn't
understand dragon talk. What they
heard was a terrible dragon ROAR.
They ran for their lives.

Four soldiers stepped out of the
woods. Herbert didn't know they were
the princess's royal guard. He grabbed the
princess to save her. The soldiers began
to shoot.

Dragons are too scaly to be hurt by arrows.
But Herbert was scared. So Herbert ran and ran. . . .

He ran straight home to his snug cave. Herbert slammed the front door and locked it.

As for the princess, she began to rant and rave. "You silly-looking dragon!" she shouted. "When my father the king finds out you've carried me away, he's going to cut off your head."

"Oh, my," thought Herbert. "What have I done?"

He opened the door so the princess could
leave.

"Oh, no," she said. "My mother told me never
to go out alone after dark. I'm staying right
here until my father comes to rescue me."

18

"Perhaps some music will cheer her up,"
thought Herbert. He turned on the radio.
But the princess shouted, "I hate dragon
music!" Then she broke the radio.

Herbert fixed a great big bowl of soup
for the princess.

"Icky, sticky dragon soup—UGH!"
cried the princess, and she threw the
bowl at Herbert.

He put clean sheets on the bed in the guest room.

But the princess screamed, "Dusty, musty dragon bed—YUCK!" Then she tore the sheets off the bed.

The princess grew more and more angry.
She smashed Herbert's fine dragon-bone china.

Then the
brave
knight saved the
fair
maiden.

She tipped over his bookcase. She
broke all of his toys. The princess carried
on all night. Herbert got very little sleep.

In the morning, there came a loud banging at the door. Poking his head out the window, Herbert saw a knight in armor. He looked brave.

"Come out and fight, you terrible dragon," shouted the knight.

Herbert was frightened. And whenever Herbert was frightened he got the hiccups. Herbert hiccuped and hiccuped. Clouds of smoke poured from his nose.

Needless to say, the brave knight galloped away.

That afternoon, the king and his army marched into Herbert's front yard—ready to attack!

One look at the cannon and the battering ram and Herbert was terrified. And whenever Herbert was terrified he began to cough.

Herbert coughed and coughed and coughed. Streams of fire and smoke poured from his nose and mouth. The king's cannon melted. The battering ram caught fire. The army turned and ran away.

"Now look what you've done, you terrible dragon!" said the princess. "You've scared my father's army away."

With that, she pushed Herbert aside and left, slamming the door behind her.

Herbert's heart was broken. He knew he had made a mess of things. "I guess I'm not cut out to be a brave knight," he thought.

For days, Herbert just sat in his cave, feeling very sad. Then an old friend dropped in for a visit.

"Herbert, have you heard the news?" he asked.

Of course, Herbert hadn't. His radio was still broken.

"It's just awful," said the friend. "After you melted down the king's cannon and broke up his army, the evil Duke of Dingbat and his men kidnapped the princess and carried her away to Castle Grouch. The king has no army to rescue his daughter."

Well, dragons usually have treasure lying around. And Herbert just happened to have a wagonload of gold in his cellar.

"I will go to the Duke of Dingbat and trade this gold for the princess," thought Herbert. "It's the least I can do."

Herbert knocked at the gate of Castle Grouch. "Hello," he called. "I'll trade you a wagonload of gold for the princess."

But the Duke of Dingbat didn't understand dragon talk. What he heard was a terrible dragon ROAR.

"A dragon has attacked!" he shouted. "Dump a ton of rocks on him."

So the duke's evil men pushed a ton of rocks off the castle wall, right on top of Herbert. Of course, Herbert wasn't hurt a bit. But Herbert was horrified. And whenever Herbert was horrified his nose tickled. And whenever his nose tickled he sneezed.

"Ah-ah-ah-ah-CHOO!!"
Herbert sneezed so hard that he blew
a huge hole in the wall of Castle Grouch.

You don't have to think very hard to
know that the duke and his men tried to
slip out the back door. But the duke had
lost his key. They were trapped.

Herbert took the princess back to her father's castle. He made the Duke of Dingbat and his men pull the wagonload of gold all the way.

You've probably guessed that Herbert was a hero. The king made him First Knight and Grand Dragon of the Kingdom.

Then the king gave a big party, with music and dancing and presents for everyone.

Herbert was a knight in armor at last. But not a *brave* knight in armor. He was still the same old timid Herbert.

Of course, nobody knew that except the princess. And she never told anyone. However, she always made sure that no one ever scared, frightened, terrified, or horrified Herbert again.

THE END